W9-CNW-129

Stevie

by John Steptoe

Harper & Row, Publishers

L. C. Number: 69-16700
ISBN 0-06-025763-6
ISBN 0-06-025764-4 (lib. bdg.)

To Marcia and Charles

One day my momma told me, "You know you're gonna have a little friend come stay with you."

And I said, "Who is it?"

And she said, "You know my friend Mrs. Mack? Well, she has to work all week and I'm gonna keep her little boy."

I asked, "For how long?"

She said, "He'll stay all week and his mother will come pick him up on Saturdays."

The next day the doorbell rang. It was a lady and a kid. He was smaller than me. I ran to my mother. "Is that them?"

They went in the kitchen but I stayed out in the hall to listen.

The little boy's name was Steven but his mother kept calling him Stevie. My name is Robert but my momma don't call me Robertie.

And so Steve moved in, with his old crybaby self. He always had to have his way. And he was greedy too. Everything he sees he wants. "Could I have somma that? Gimme this." Man!

Since he was littler than me, while I went to school he used to stay home and play with my toys.

I wished his mother would bring somma *his* toys over here to break up.

I used to get so mad at my mother when I came home after school. "Momma, can't you watch him and tell him to leave my stuff alone?"

Then he used to like to get up on my bed to look out the window and leave his dirty footprints all over my bed. And my momma never said nothin' to him.

And on Saturdays when his mother comes to pick him up, he always tries to act cute just cause his mother is there.

He picked up my airplane and I told him not to bother it. He thought I wouldn't say nothin' to him in front of his mother.

I could never go anywhere without my mother sayin' "Take Stevie with you now."

"But why I gotta take him everywhere I go?" I'd say.

"Now if you were stayin' with someone you wouldn't want them to treat you mean," my mother told me. "Why don't you and Stevie try to play nice?"

Yeah, but I always been nice to him with his old

spoiled self. He's always gotta have his way anyway. I had to take him out to play with me and my friends.

"Is that your brother, Bobby?" they'd ask me.

"No."

"Is that your cousin?"

"No! He's just my friend and he's stayin' at my house and my mother made me bring him."

"Ha, ha. You gotta baby-sit! Bobby the baby-sitter!"

"Aw, be quiet. Come on, Steve. See! Why you gotta make all my friends laugh for?"

"Ha, ha. Bobby the baby-sitter," my friends said.

"Hey, come on, y'all, let's go play in the park. You comin', Bobby?" one of my friends said.

"Naw, my momma said he can't go in the park cause the last time he went he fell and hurt his knee, with his old stupid self."

And then they left.

"You see? You see! I can't even play with my friends. Man! Come on."

"I'm sorry, Robert. You don't like me, Robert? I'm sorry," Stevie said.

"Aw, be quiet. That's okay," I told him.

One time when my daddy was havin' company I was just sittin' behind the couch just listenin' to them talk and make jokes and drink beer. And I wasn't makin' no noise. They didn't even know I was there!

Then here comes Stevie with his old loud self. Then when my father heard him, he yelled at *me* and told me to go upstairs.

Just cause of Stevie.

Sometimes people get on your nerves and they don't mean it or nothin' but they just bother you. Why I gotta put up with him? My momma only had one kid. I used to have a lot of fun before old stupid came to live with us.

One Saturday Steve's mother and father came to my house to pick him up like always. But they said that they were gonna move away and that Stevie wasn't gonna come back anymore.

So then he left. The next mornin' I got up to watch cartoons and I fixed two bowls of corn flakes. Then I just remembered that Stevie wasn't here.

Sometimes we had a lot of fun runnin' in and out of the house. Well, I guess my bed will stay clean from now on. But that wasn't so bad. He couldn't help it cause he was stupid.

I remember the time I ate the last piece of cake in the breadbox and blamed it on him.

We used to play Cowboys and Indians on the stoop.

I remember when I was doin' my homework I used to try to teach him what I had learned. He could write his name pretty good for his age.

I remember the time we played boogie man and we hid under the covers with Daddy's flashlight.

And that time we was playin' in the park under the bushes and we found these two dead rats and one was brown and one was black.

And him and me and my friends used to cook mickies or marshmallows in the park.

We used to have some good times together.

I think he liked my momma better than his own, cause he used to call his mother "Mother" and he called my momma "Mommy."

Aw, no! I let my corn flakes get soggy thinkin' about him.

He was a nice little guy.
He was kinda like a little brother.
Little Stevie.